check out the inside
cover –

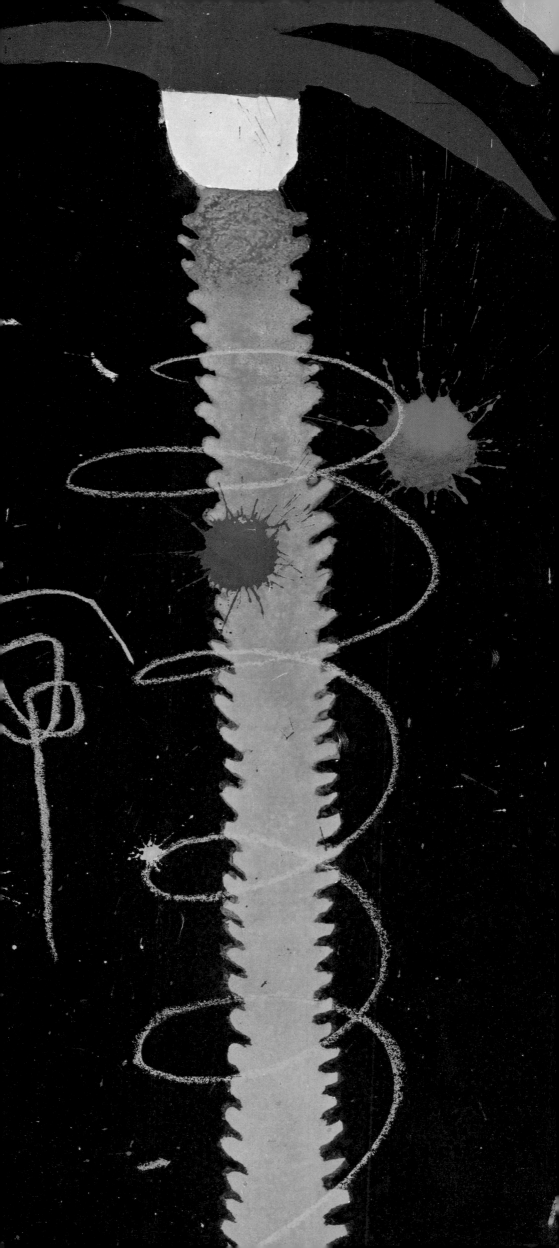

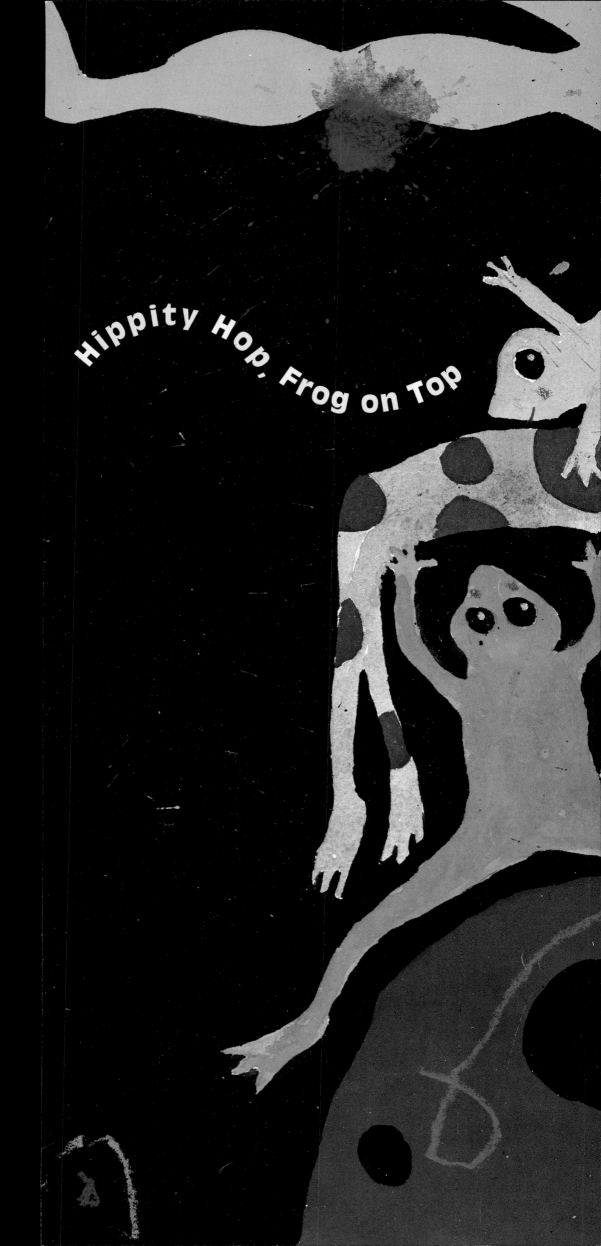

Hippity Hop, Frog on Top

BY Natasha Wing

ILLUSTRATED BY DeLoss McGraw

Hippity Hop, Frog on Top

SIMON & SCHUSTER BOOKS FOR YOUNG READERS
Published by Simon & Schuster
Sydney   Tokyo   Singapore
New York   London   Toronto

SIMON & SCHUSTER BOOKS FOR YOUNG READERS
1230 Avenue of the Americas, New York, New York 10020
Text copyright © 1994 by Natasha Wing
Illustrations copyright © 1994 by DeLoss McGraw
SIMON & SCHUSTER BOOKS FOR YOUNG READERS
is a trademark of Simon & Schuster.
Typographic design by Joy Chu.
The text of this book is set in Antique Olive Bold.
The illustrations were done in gouache and colored pencil.
Manufactured in the United States of America

10 9 8 7 6 5 4 3 2 1

Library of Congress Cataloging-in-Publication Data
Wing, Natasha. Hippity hop, frog on top/by Natasha Wing;
illustrated by DeLoss McGraw. Summary: Ten curious frogs trying to
see what's on the other side of a wall illustrate the numbers from
one to ten. [1. Frogs—Fiction. 2. Counting.] I. McGraw, DeLoss, ill.
II. Title. PZ7.W72825Hi 1994 [E]—dc20 93-11473 CIP AC
ISBN 0-671-87045-9

To Dan and our lucky frog — N.W.

*To my three favorite
architects —
Giotto di Bodone,
Aldo Rossi
and my dad,
DeLoss L. McGraw* — D.M.

One big bullfrog came to a wall. "I wonder what's on the other side," he croaked.

He hopped on a rock.
He still could not
see over.

Hippity hop, frog on top.
1 frog, one frog tall,
could not see over the wall.

Along bounced a spotted frog.

Bullfrog called to him.
"Will you help me?" he asked.
"I want to know what's on
the other side of this wall."

Hippity hop, frog on top.
2 frogs, two frogs tall,
could not see over the wall.

A frog with wide webbed feet
plip-plopped beside the rock.
"What are you
two doing?"
the frog asked.

"We're trying to see what's on
the other side of this wall,"
croaked Bullfrog. "We
could use your help."

Hippity hop, frog on top.
3 frogs, three frogs tall,
could not see
over the wall.

A frog with strong legs leaped over the pile.

"Can you jump higher than this wall,"
croaked Bullfrog, "and tell us what's
on the other side?"
The frog jumped and jumped
and jumped. He could not jump
high enough.

Hippity hop, frog on top.
frogs, four frogs tall,
could not see
over the wall.

"Ribbit, ribbit," said a frog with a puffed-up throat. "What have we here?"

"We're trying to see what's on the other side of this wall," croaked Bullfrog. "Will you help us?"

Hippity hop, frog on top.
5 frogs, five frogs tall, could not see over the wall.

A frog with a long,
sticky tongue
caught a fly and
gulped it down.
"Why are you all piled up
like that?" he asked.
Bullfrog croaked, "We want
to see what's on the other
side of this wall. Care to
take a look?"

Hippity hop, frog on top.
6 frogs, six frogs tall,
could not see over the wall.

"Are you all trying
to stay warm?" asked
a frog covered
with mud.

"We're just trying
to see what's on the
other side of this wall,"
croaked Bullfrog. "You
are welcome to join us."

Hippity hop, frog on top.
7 frogs, seven frogs tall,
could not see over the wall.

"This must be a great place to sun!" said a striped frog.

"Jump on top and you'll get the
sunniest spot," croaked
Bullfrog. "And while you're up
there, tell us what's on the
other side of
this wall."

Hippity hop, frog on top.
8 frogs, eight frogs tall,
could not see over the wall.

A frog with bulging eyes said, "What do I see here?"

Bullfrog croaked, "We're trying to find out what's on the other side of this wall. Maybe you could take a peek."

Hippity hop, frog on top.
9 frogs, nine frogs tall, could not see over the wall.

"Can I play leapfrog, too?"
peeped a tiny tree frog.

"You sure can,"
croaked Bullfrog.

"Just leap
on the heap
and tell us what's on the
other side of this wall."

Hippity hop,
frog on top.
10 frogs against
the wall, now
the pile is plenty tall.

"What do you see? What do you see?" asked the nine frogs in harmony.
"A hungry alligator coming at me!"

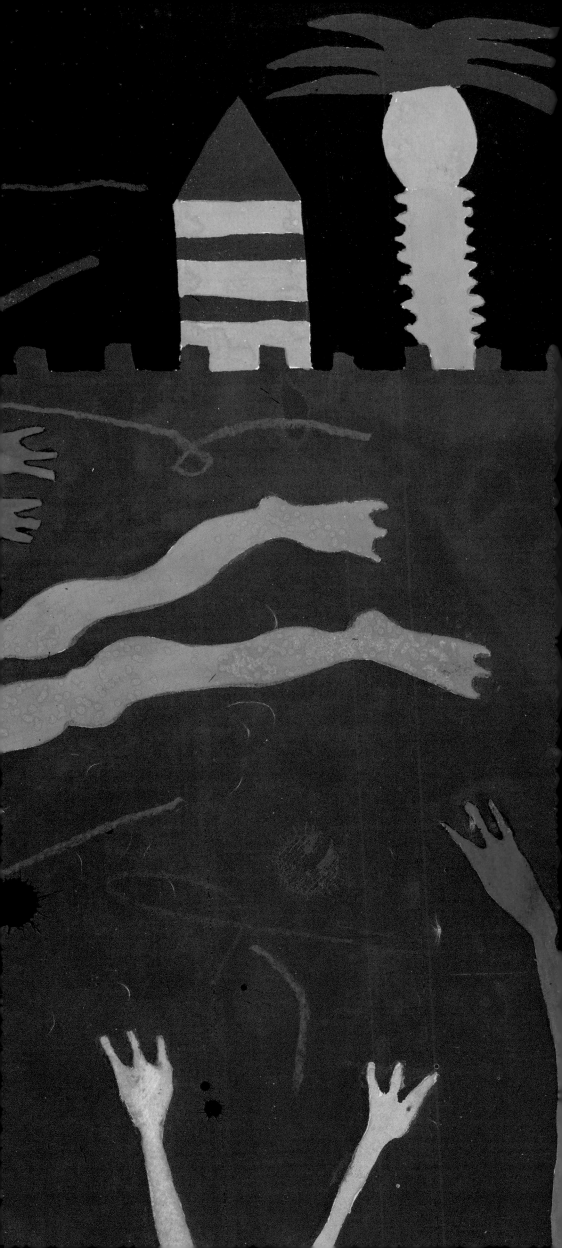

Hippity hop, frogs *ker-plop*.
Now there are no frogs
against the wall.